# Experimenting with Surface Tension and Bubbles

## Alan Ward

*Illustrated by Zena Flax*

CHELSEA JUNIORS
A division of Chelsea House Publishers
New York · Philadelphia

# Contents

First Printing

1 3 5 7 9 8 6 4 2

ISBN 0-7910-1513-0

# *Preface*

I discovered bubbles when I was a young adult – and found out what I had missed as a child. From a second-hand book shop, I bought a first edition (1900) of *Soap Bubbles and the Forces Which Mould Them* – a course of three lectures delivered to a young audience in the London Institution on the afternoons of 30 December 1889 and 1 and 3 January 1890. The author and lecturer was C V Boys and his fame and especially his little book are known today.

In the manner of Professor Boys, I have begun this exploration of bubbles with some explanation of surface tension. This helps us to understand how a bubble is shaped by such an improbable "skin" as one made with water – a fact worthy of the description "liquid engineering". The experiments on bubbles in the main part of the book are invitations to science drama – so practice them well. Bubbles will remind you that the sweetest pleasures in life are brief – they are most beautiful with "rainbow colors" just before they vanish.

You should have no difficulty in getting together the apparatus needed for the experiments. The materials are inexpensive and most of them can be found in your home. You can buy the perforated zinc metal for the sailors' boat from a hardware store. Do be very careful when you are using dangerous materials like wire, pliers, hammer, nails and glass. Always set up candles in a dish of sand – and don't burn your fingers, let alone the room where you are working. The candle will not set fire to the sand if it should fall over. Always read through the instructions completely, before starting work. It is wise to make a list of the materials you will need. Remember that a scientist is a patient person. Don't expect the experiments to work well the first time. You need to practice the slight skills needed for success, and you will feel very pleased with yourself when your patience is rewarded. You will enjoy demonstrating your accomplishments to your friends – and teaching them, too.

# What is surface tension?

Fill a small glass with water – up to the brim. See how many pins you can put through the surface without spilling any water. As the pins pile up underwater, notice what is happening to the surface.

It bulges above the brim of the glass, forming a curve like a thin dome. The water acts as if it has a skin stopping it from overflowing. Eventually the surface does appear to "burst" and some water runs away.

You can repeat the test, using pennies. But does the water really have a skin?

## Why it works

Water, like all substances, consists of particles called molecules, that are too small to see. These water molecules attract each other with a force called cohesion. This explains why water "sticks together".

Most of the little forces between the molecules cancel each other out – because the molecules are surrounded by other water molecules. But at the surface there are no effective forces to pull on the molecules from outside the water. (You can ignore the effect of air molecules.) So the attraction is stronger between the surface molecules and the ones below. The surface molecules are rather like people trying to force themselves into the edge of a crowd.

This effect of cohesion is called surface tension ("tightness") and makes the water act as if it had an elastic skin. In fact, there is no such "skin" in the sense of something like the skin on boiled milk that can be skimmed off.

# It is possible for water to support solid steel

Fill a drinking glass with water.

Hold out flat a **blunt** razor-blade, held by the short edges between finger and thumb. Practice dropping the steel blade in this position, by opening your fingers.

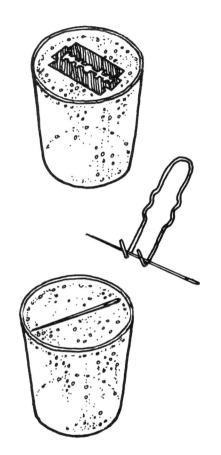

The blade is made of a material that is nearly eight times denser ("heavier") than water. It is also solid, so it should sink. Yet, when you let it fall from a short distance above the water in the glass, the blade apparently floats.

But the blade is not floating in a strictly scientific sense. It is simply *resting* on the surface tension.

Bend up the ends of a hairpin to make a holder for a clean sewing needle. With care, you can lower the needle on to clean water so that it, too, rests on the surface.

Also try resting a clean needle on a small piece of paper towel. The paper sinks, leaving the needle on the surface.

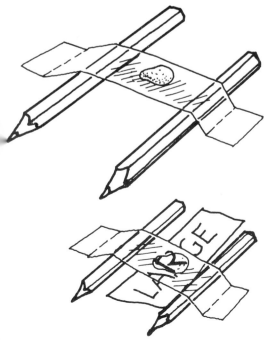

# A waterdrop microscope

Rest two pencils on the table with a gap of 3 inches between them. Stretch a strip of wide sticky tape across the pencils and fix the ends of the tape to the table. Put a drop of water on the glossy side of the tape. Surface tension holds the drop together and the force of gravity flattens it against the tape, to form a water lens.

Small objects, such as a postage stamp or a newspaper picture, placed under the lens are magnified.

What happens to the lens if you touch it with the end of a matchstick that has been dipped in washing-up liquid?

# Weakening surface tension

Sprinkle talcum-powder on to the surface of some clean water in a glass bowl.

Where the powder rests, touch it with a finger that you have wetted with detergent (washing-up liquid). The particles of powder seem to explode apart, and then start to sink.

Molecules of detergent spread over the surface, covering the water and therefore destroying the water's surface tension. The surface tension of the detergent is weak, so the talcum-powder is pulled apart by the stronger pull from unpolluted water at the edge of the bowl.

**Note** Talcum-powder, being greasy, does not adhere (stick) directly to water molecules. Another effect of the detergent is to form molecular links between water and the powder, therefore letting the denser-than-water powder break through into the main body of water (in other words, to sink).

Look also at page 14.

## Triangle test

Cut three 4-inch lengths of plastic drinking-straws. Use another straw to help you to float the pieces on the surface of clean, still water – and to form them into a triangular raft.

Touch the water in the middle of the triangle with a finger wetted with detergent. Surface tension inside the triangle is reduced, making it possible for the stronger pulls from the clean water to "explode" the triangle.

Clean everything before repeating this beautiful test.

# Surface tension "motor" boats

Put clean water into a clean plastic plant-pot tray (measuring about 6 x 24 in). At one end of the tray, float a polystyrene food dish (approximately 5 x 9 in). If you wish you can give the food container a balsa-wood mast and a paper flag.

Touch the water between the tray and the model boat with a detergent-wet finger. Instantly, the vessel is pulled along by the stronger surface tension on its opposite end.

Everything, including your hands, must be washed free of detergent before this (and all the other detergent experiments) will work again.

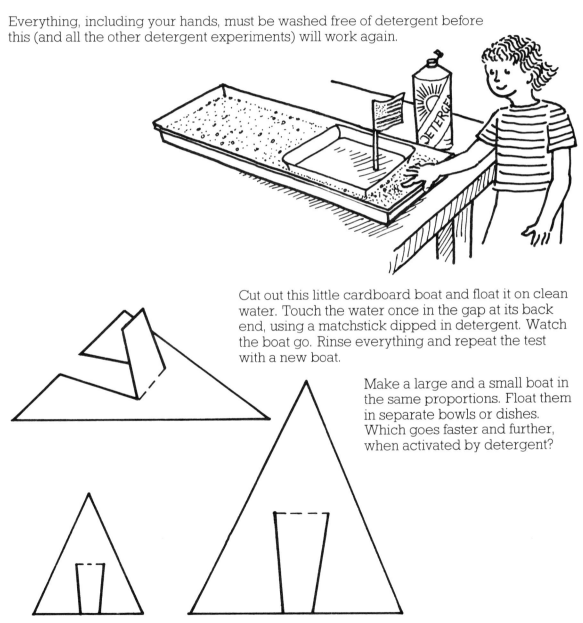

Cut out this little cardboard boat and float it on clean water. Touch the water once in the gap at its back end, using a matchstick dipped in detergent. Watch the boat go. Rinse everything and repeat the test with a new boat.

Make a large and a small boat in the same proportions. Float them in separate bowls or dishes. Which goes faster and further, when activated by detergent?

# The strength of surface tension

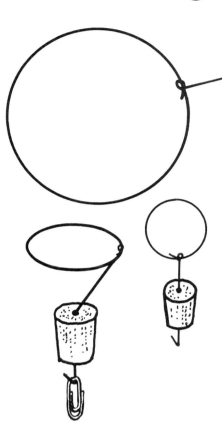

Make a special float called a "bobbing frame" that can be trapped underwater by the force of surface tension.

From thick fuse-wire, form a 2-inch-diameter ring on a stem about 4 inches long. You can shape the ring around a bottle.

Pass the stem of the wire through a hole that is bored in a small cork, using a thin nail – and bend up the end of the stem, under the cork, to make a hook.

Bend down the ring and bend the stem above the cork, so that the ring and the top of the cork are horizontal ("flat") and – when you are looking directly down on the object – the cork is immediately under the center of the ring.

You have to get the bobbing frame to only just float. Do this by hanging paperclips on the hook. While the cork is barely afloat, the stem with its ring must be above the level of the water.

## Testing

When you push the frame underwater in a wide jar (you could use a plastic lemonade bottle with its top cut off), it must stay submerged, with its ring pressing up against the under-surface. The surface may even bulge slightly upwards.

Then, if you use a bent-wire hook to pull the ring gently up through the surface, the frame bobs through and floats with its ring in the air.

You have proved that surface tension is a force to be reckoned with from *inside* a liquid.

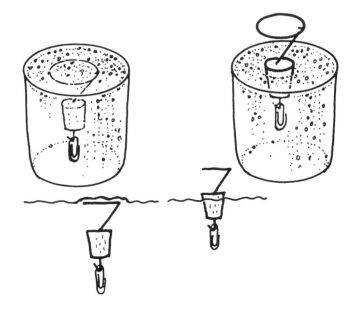

# A balance for comparing surface tensions

Form a stirrup shape from stiff wire and fix it in a cork that is inserted in a bottle – that will support the balance. Push a needle through the middle of a thin wooden rod, 24 inches long, and balance this stick in the stirrup.

From fuse-wire make a perfect ring, 3 inches in diameter. Hang this by equal cotton threads from a small pin pushed into one end of the stick.

Make a balance pan from an aluminum cake cup, and suspend this from the opposite end of the stick. A piece of bent iron wire, straddled over the stick and which can be slid to and fro, acts as an adjustable rider – to help you get the apparatus to balance, before doing tests.

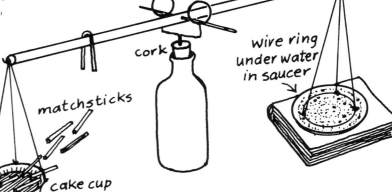

## Testing

Push the wire ring under the surface of some clean water held in a saucer. Put one or two matchsticks into the balance pan. Their weight (the pull of gravity on them) will force the ring up against the water's surface – like your bobbing frame. Keep adding matchsticks until their weight makes the ring break up through the surface.

Compare surface tensions of:    cold water                    **How many matches?**
                                         hot water
                                         soapy water
                                         gasoline
                                         carbon tetrachloride

**Warning: Matches are dangerous. Gasoline catches fire easily. Carbon tetrachloride evaporates to form a poisonous gas – so use it in a well-ventilated place.**

Wash out the saucer before each test.

# Tricks with surface tension

## *How to pour water along a string*

Bore a small hole in the lip of a cheap plastic jug. Do this using the end of a wire which you have heated in a candle flame. (**Stand the candle in a dish of sand, for safety.**) Thread a piece of string through the hole and tie a knot in the end of the string, to stop it from slipping out.

Fill the jug with water and wet the string, but do not make the string too wet.

Hold the jug in one hand while you stretch the string between the lip of the jug and where you have tied the other end of the string to a finger of your other hand. Hold this finger over a bowl.

Keep the string tight. Slope the string down towards your finger. Then, gently, pour the water on to the string.

Like magic, the water trickles along the string – and does not fall off – to drain from your finger, into the bowl.

Water adheres to the wet string. Cohesion holds the water together and surface tension forms a pipe-like "skin" for the water to flow through.

# Squeeze play

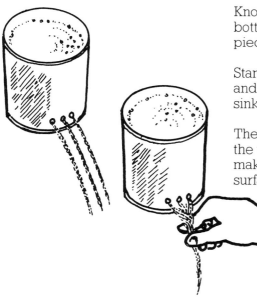

Knock three small nail holes, side by side, near the bottom end of an empty tin. Cover the holes with a piece of sticky tape, while you fill the tin with water.

Stand the tin on the edge of a sink. Pull off the tape and let three jets of water flow, side by side, into the sink.

Then, using clean fingers, act as if you are squeezing the water-jets together. Apparently you really do make the jets go together . . . . A combined "skin" of surface tension does the trick.

# Instant shipwreck

Have you ever heard of the sailors who went to sea in a sieve? (How silly, you might imagine – a sieve is filled with holes . . . )

Make a metal sieve by bending up the sides of a piece of perforated zinc metal – used to let air into outdoor food stores, without letting in flies. Perforated zinc can be obtained from a hardware store.

This is the sailors' crazy boat. You can rest it, *very gently*, on still, clean water in a bowl. The water bulges up through the hundreds of holes, but does not wet the metal and is stopped from leaking into the boat by surface tension.

Cut out some paper sailors and gently sit them on board. Then, where a tiny drop of water bulges, touch it with a match dipped in detergent.

You have an instant shipwreck…

# Insects of the water's surface

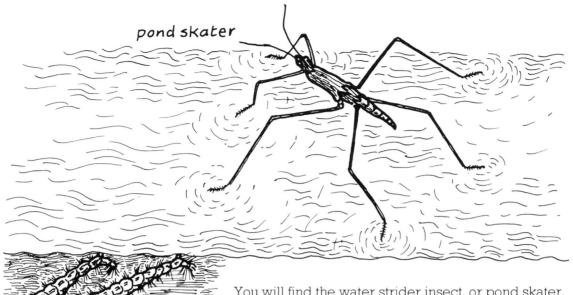

pond skater

mosquito larvae cling under the surface film – their rear-end breathing tubes push through into the air

You will find the water strider insect, or pond skater, living on the water film of surface tension, on ponds and quiet rivers. Its six feet are covered with tiny hairs that are not wettable by water. This means that water does not stick to them. If it did, the delicate but athletic insect would be pulled into the main body of the water, where it would be unable to move and hunt as it needs to, to survive.

If you look closely, you can observe the dents made by the insect's feet, as the pull of its weight forces it against the water's surface.

Did you notice how the water's surface was dented when you tried the razor-blade test?

If another insect accidentally falls into the water, a pond skater can detect its struggles, as vibrations rippling the surface. There are vibration-detectors between its leg joints. Pond skaters even communicate with each other by making vibratory signals on the surface.

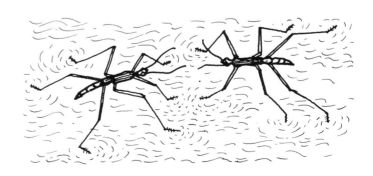

A pond skater feeds by using its complicated mouthparts to stab another insect, before injecting a substance that anesthetizes and, after some minutes, liquifies the soft body parts of its prey. Then it sucks out the food and casts away the insect's empty body shell.

If you catch a pond skater and put it in a large bowl, perhaps you can watch it feed, when you drop in ants or plant bugs.

Also, watch how it moves about by rowing itself along and steering with its oar-like legs.

# A model insect

Devise a model pond skater. Form the body from a used matchstick. Make six legs from pieces of thin fuse-wire. They should all be about 2 inches long. Spread out the feet, to get them to rest flat when you stand the model on a level surface.

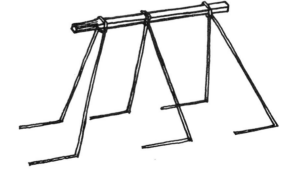

Dip the feet in some candle wax that you have melted safely in a tin lid held over a candle flame. (**Hold the lid with pliers.**) The wax makes the feet non-wettable, or water-repellent.

When you lower the model on to the surface of clean water in a dish, your mock water strider-cum-pond skater should dent the surface film.

What would you expect to happen if you polluted the water with a few drops of liquid detergent? (Try it.)

# How a detergent works

Fresh water does not wash away fat or grease from your hands. Oily substances repel water. Therefore, it does not wet, or stick to them. This is a problem, because dirt usually contains some grease or oiliness. Something is needed to join with both greasy dirt and water, so that the dirt can be washed away. Detergents, such as soaps and washing-up liquids, can do this.

head

tail

Detergent molecules can be imagined as being like tiny heads with long tails. The heads are "water-loving" and adhere to water. The tails are "grease-loving" and, although they are repelled by water molecules, will stick to molecules of grease, oil, wax and fat. Detergent molecules can be thought of as molecular links or "hooks".

Try to spread water on waxed paper (for instance, the packaging material that holds your breakfast Corn Flakes). The water just forms blobs and drops. It spreads, however, when you mix in some washing-up liquid.

To see how added detergent helps water to pull oily matter into small pieces that can be rinsed away, shake up some salad oil in a jar of water – then add a few drops of detergent, before shaking again. The oil is broken up (emulsified) into silvery droplets.

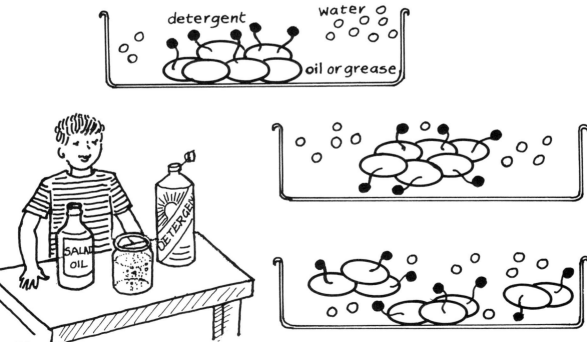

# Wetter water

Yes, what the advertisements claim is true –
detergents do make water "wetter than wet". By
helping water to adhere to greasy materials,
detergents enable water to penetrate the air spaces
in washing, to make the dirt-removing processes
easier. (In a washing-machine, the sheets and clothes
are rotated and churned up, to improve the action
even more.)

A duck can float because it makes its feathers oily,
by rubbing in oil from a gland situated near its tail.
The oil repels water. Air, trapped in cell-like spaces
amongst its feathers, keeps a duck floating high and
dry above the water.

To get some idea of what might
happen if you were foolish
enough to pollute a duck pond
with detergent, float a screwed-
up ball of waxed paper in a bowl.
Then add some washing-up
liquid to the water . . .

Polythene plastic bags are also
water-repellent. Ball up a piece
of a clear plastic bag, as well as
you can. It floats quite well –
before you make the water
wetter with detergent.

# What is a bubble?

You have observed globular drops of water resting on waxy leaves, after a thunderstorm. The drops are held in shape by films of surface tension. They do not lose their shapes by spreading, because the wax repels the water.

Perhaps it might be possible to blow air into a drop of water, to make the surface grow into a larger elastic covering – and form a water bubble . . . . When you run water from the tap into a washbowl, small bubbles do occur, but they are soon destroyed.

The forces between water molecules are so great that bubbles forming from pure water are torn apart by their own surface tension.

But the surface tension is weakened when you mix detergent with water. Detergent molecules cover the surface, enabling it to stretch without breaking.

Extra detergent molecules needed to line expanding surfaces come from amongst spare ones in the water. This happens rapidly because the tail ends of detergent molecules (the "grease-loving" ends, that also "hate" water) are water-repellent and so they are forced to the surface.

A bubble consists of a sandwich-like covering, or envelope, enclosing a gas (usually air). Detergent molecules form stretchy outer and inner surfaces that contain water (which holds the envelope together) and detergent.

● ～   detergent molecule

O    water molecule

# A mixture for making bubbles

Make up a bubble-blowing mixture by gently stirring half a cupful of washing-up liquid into ten cupfuls of warm water. While doing this, do not make masses of small bubbles called suds.

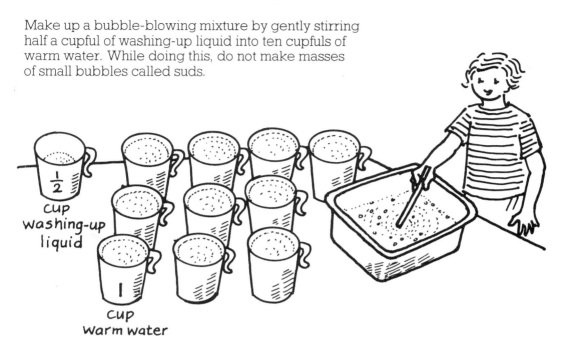

$\frac{1}{2}$ cup washing-up liquid

1 cup warm water

If you make a rough tube, by curling your fingers, and dip the hand in bubble mixture, you should be able to use this very basic "pipe" to blow sizeable bubbles.

A bubble forms when you force air from your breath to stretch the elastic bubble mixture "sandwich" that is supported by your wet fingers.

# Floppy films and super bubbles

Using wire from a coat-hanger make a big ring, by bending the wire around a large tin. Twist the ends of the wire together, with pliers, but leave a straight bit of wire to use as a handle.

Dip the ring into a small tea-tray, or dinner plate, containing bubble mixture. Pull out the ring, avoiding suds. It will hold a shimmering detergent film.

Anything wet, such as a finger – or even a stream of water poured from a jug, will penetrate this film, without breaking it. You can even hit the film with a well-wetted hammer . . .

The wet surface of anything coming into contact with the film on the frame actually becomes part of the detergent film, during these magical tests. That is why the film does not break.

Shake a wire-supported film up and down and watch it stretch and flop to and fro, pushed by the air.

If you use a mixture of detergent and water containing much more detergent than water, it is possible to create giant bubbles, by moving the wet frame through the air. Go outside on a breezy day and let the gusts of wind do your work for you.

Also try using bubble mixtures sold in toyshops.

# Bubble "pipes"

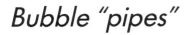

Make a bubble pipe by cutting four 1-inch-long slits in the end of a plastic drinking-straw. Bend the divisions outwards, to form a flower-like object.

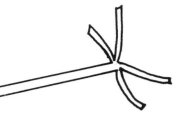

Dip this prepared end into bubble mixture. Put the other end between your sealed lips. Slope the pipe downwards, and gently blow . . . . A small bubble forms from a drop of mixture, and clings to your straw pipe.

Jerk the pipe slightly, to shake the bubble free.

Make a Super Bubble Pipe by cutting the bottom end off a plastic bottle, such as a washing-up liquid bottle. Cut eight short slits at the wide end of the tube, bending aside the divisions, as before.

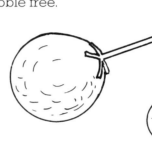

After dipping the bottom end in bubble mixture, blow steadily into the mouth of the bottle, to stretch the film of liquid caught just below. You will soon learn how to "pump" several breaths into the pipe, to create a giant bubble. (Take fresh breaths through your nose, without taking your lips away from the mouthpiece.)

Tilt the pipe a little to one side and jerk it slightly, to shake the big bubble free. Watch it wobble as it falls.

With a little practice you will easily master these minor skills.

# Minimal surfaces

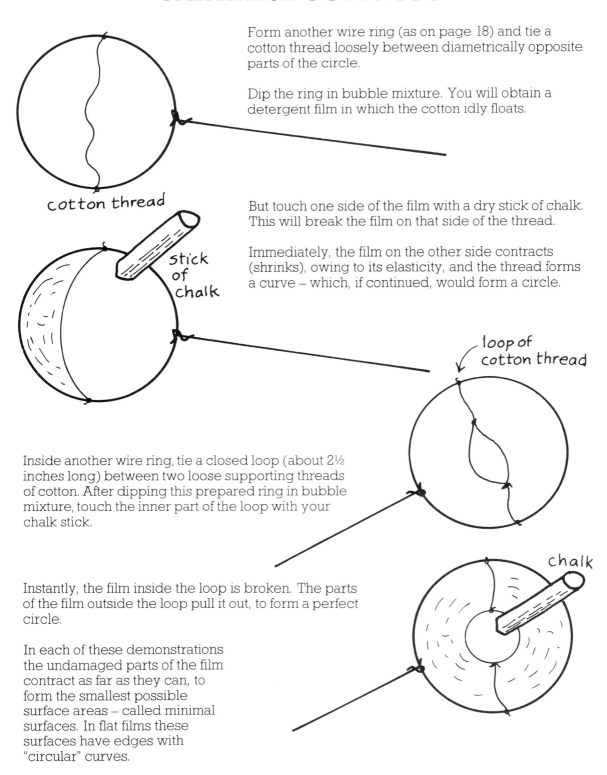

Form another wire ring (as on page 18) and tie a cotton thread loosely between diametrically opposite parts of the circle.

Dip the ring in bubble mixture. You will obtain a detergent film in which the cotton idly floats.

cotton thread

But touch one side of the film with a dry stick of chalk. This will break the film on that side of the thread.

Immediately, the film on the other side contracts (shrinks), owing to its elasticity, and the thread forms a curve – which, if continued, would form a circle.

stick of chalk

loop of cotton thread

Inside another wire ring, tie a closed loop (about 2½ inches long) between two loose supporting threads of cotton. After dipping this prepared ring in bubble mixture, touch the inner part of the loop with your chalk stick.

Instantly, the film inside the loop is broken. The parts of the film outside the loop pull it out, to form a perfect circle.

In each of these demonstrations the undamaged parts of the film contract as far as they can, to form the smallest possible surface areas – called minimal surfaces. In flat films these surfaces have edges with "circular" curves.

chalk

# Why an ordinary bubble is shaped like a sphere

Keep your fingertip over the narrow end of a plastic funnel, *wetted inside*. Dip the other end of the funnel in bubble mixture, to capture a detergent film.

Notice what happens when you take away your finger. The circular film contracts – and slides up the *wet* interior of the narrowing tube.

This experience will help you to understand what is happening to the envelope that surrounds a bubble.

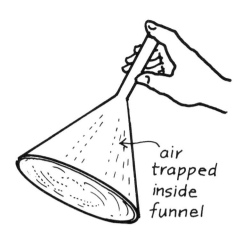

air trapped inside funnel

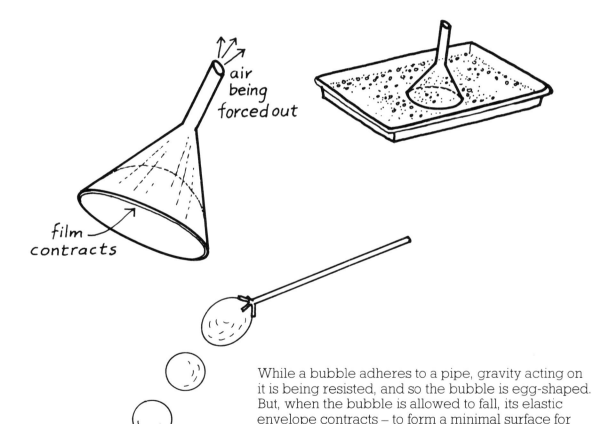

air being forced out

film contracts

While a bubble adheres to a pipe, gravity acting on it is being resisted, and so the bubble is egg-shaped. But, when the bubble is allowed to fall, its elastic envelope contracts – to form a minimal surface for the mass of air which it contains. *The surface tends to be sphere-shaped.*

Freely falling water drops are also spheres. Can you guess why?

# More films in frames

Another way to make detergent films for experiments is to use an apparatus made by threading a loop of thin string between two plastic straws or peashooter tubes.

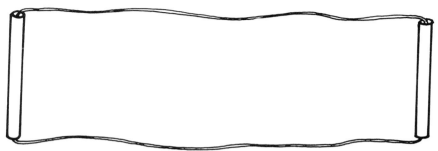

Wet your fingers before grasping the plastic handles of this frame. Dip the frame in bubble mixture. It will be convenient to have the mixture in a tray, or even in a bath. When you remove the wetted apparatus and pull the strings, you will have a large detergent film.

By keeping the strings tight, while raising each hand alternately, you can produce a wave in the film that passes to and fro.

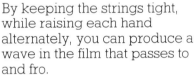

By pulling the frame upwards, from below waist level, you can catch enough air by a stretching film, to make a very big bubble. Bring the handles together to release this bubble. (It might be a good idea to make up a stronger mixture, if you want enormous bubbles.)

# Cubic bubbles

With special methods, it is possible to create cube-shaped bubbles, but their filmy envelopes always need some sort of support. Indeed, the faces of larger cubes will be curved and, therefore, they are not true cubes.

Put some bubble mixture in a tray. Rest a sheet of perspex (or, less safely, glass) on four corks standing like table-legs inside the tray. There will be a gap between the perspex and the surface of the liquid.

Use a peashooter or other plastic tube, to blow bubbles under the covering. The bubbles will be squashed together and have flat surfaces where they touch.

Notice that, generally speaking, only three surfaces meet along an edge (forming three equal angles of 120°). *You might get a little cubic bubble squashed in amongst the others.*

Use a cube-shaped frame, roughly made from twelve lengths of wire (twisted at the corners, using pliers), to make a good cubic bubble.

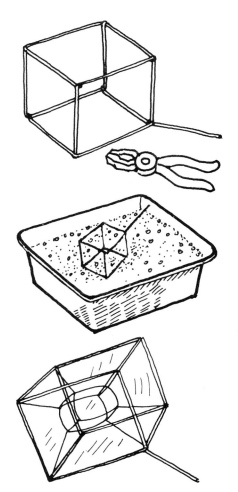

Dip the frame in a dish of bubble mixture. When you pull it out, it contains a pattern of joined films like this:

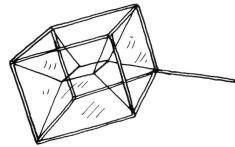

Dip in the frame again – to trap some air under the square film in the middle. When you bring out the frame this time (passing it through the floating bubble made from the air under the square), you get a cubic bubble.

# The super bubble

Blow a big bubble with the Super Bubble Pipe. To stop it from contracting and forcing out the air when you take away your mouth, put a finger over the opening. If your finger is too small, put your other hand over the hole.

(Or you could keep the original stopper of a pipe made from a washing-up liquid bottle – and just plug the little hole, after blowing your bubble.)

Hold out the bubble pipe and study your bubble as it hangs there before you. Notice how the liquid drains down inside the envelope – to form a dripping drop on the bottom of the bubble.

Shake the pipe and jerk it up and down, to see how wobbly a bubble can be.

Tilt the pipe to one side and jerk it upwards, to release the bubble. Being denser ("heavier") than the surrounding air, because it is made from compressed air and water, your bubble is pulled down by the force of gravity.

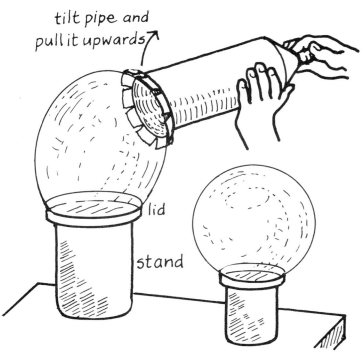

tilt pipe and
pull it upwards

lid

stand

## A bubble-stand

You can make a stand for supporting a bubble, by putting a *wetted* plastic lid or small saucer on top of a plastic bottle with its top cut off.

To put a bubble on this stand, lower the bubble on to the wet lid or saucer and let it stick there. Then, to leave the bubble behind, tilt the pipe and pull it smartly away.

A bubble on a stand is ideal for observation and for certain bubble tricks – as we shall see.

# What to look for in a bubble

Notice the reflections in a bubble. Those on the bulging (convex) outer surface of the envelope will be upright. Those on the hollow (concave) inner surface are upside-down. Study the reflections of a candle, safely set up, in a dark room.

As a bubble evaporates and gets thinner, rainbow colors appear. These become most brilliant just before the bubble bursts, scattering droplets of moisture about itself.

Notice the dark swirls in the envelope, just before self-destruction.

Bubbles last longest in a damp, cold atmosphere. Warm, dry conditions are not ideal for your bubble experiments, but will not prevent limited success. Probably the electrical condition of the atmosphere is also a factor affecting your tests.

# Why you see colors in a bubble

One of the ways scientists think about light is as a series of waves, or ripples.

A single wave has a crest (top) and a trough (bottom).

The distance between two wave crests in a continuous wave system is the wave-length.

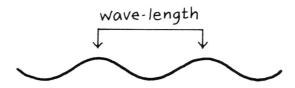

wave-length

The number of complete waves that pass a point, per second, is called the frequency.

frequency=4

time: one second

Sunlight consists of a mixture of different wave-lengths, each connected with a different color.

# Light wave interference

If, by chance, two wave systems having the same wave-length overlap, two things can happen:

The crests and troughs can overlap exactly – in which case they reinforce each other (combine) to produce a stronger wave.

Or crests can overlap troughs, cancelling each other out, to produce a flat wave.

The waves are said to interfere with each other, to produce either constructive or destructive interference.

With light of a certain frequency, constructive interference produces the effect of bright color in your mind. But destructive interference produces an impression of no color (darkness).

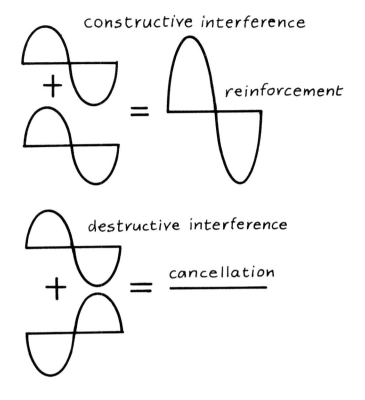

constructive interference

reinforcement

destructive interference

cancellation

Colors in nature are usually the result of mixtures of wave-lengths acting on your eyes. The wave mixture from sunlight is visible as white.

When sunlight hits a detergent film, such as the envelope of a bubble, some light is reflected from the outer surface and some from the inner surface. Most of the light passes through the film – that is why a bubble is transparent.

Through interference effects, different wave-lengths reflected from a bubble do not reach your eyes. Therefore you see colors other than white – the colors of the rainbow.

These interference effects are seen when a film is more or less as thin as the wave-lengths of light. This explains why the colors in a bubble look brightest when it has become very thin, through drainage and evaporation.

Colors appear, alter and disappear in a bubble because the thickness of the envelope is not the same everywhere and is constantly changing. Complicated sequences of constructive and destructive interference amongst the light waves cause the beautiful color transformations and mysterious swirls of darkness that you admire.

# Pressure in a bubble

Obviously the air inside a bubble is at greater pressure than the air outside it – because the bubble envelope is elastic. The bubble contracts, to squeeze and compress the air it holds.

Here is a puzzle that is not so obvious:

The picture shows two bubbles supported by wet yogurt pots which are connected by peashooter mouthpieces that are being held together. Air inside these bubbles is under pressure.

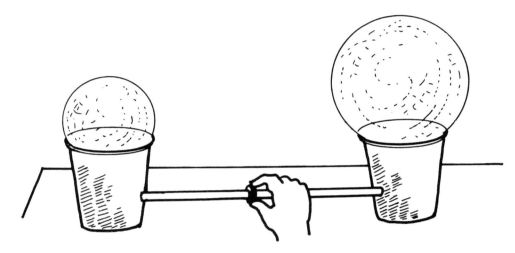

1   Will air be forced from the smaller into the larger bubble?

2   Will air be forced from the larger into the smaller bubble?

3   Guess what both bubbles should look like in about a minute's time.

**Hint** Before answering, experiment with a rubber balloon. Is it easier to inflate the balloon with breath when you start to blow, or just before you stop blowing? You could also study how the balloon whizzes around the room when you let it go – and the effect on little pieces of torn-up paper of the "wind" made by the escaping air.

If you think about the experiences with a balloon, you might come to the conclusion that pressure inside might be greatest when the balloon is small.

Also think about a gymnast on a trampoline.

The greater the curvature under the gymnast's feet, the greater the force that the trampoline is capable of exerting on them – and the higher the gymnast is going to rise.

## Answer to the bubbles problem

The small bubble gets smaller, forcing the big bubble to get bigger.

Small bubbles are more curved than larger ones. The more curved a bubble is, the greater the force exerted by its envelope on the air inside.

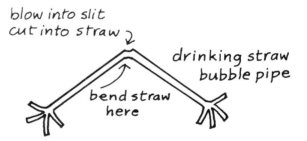

blow into slit
cut into straw

drinking straw
bubble pipe

bend straw
here

Use this apparatus, made from a single plastic straw, to confirm that the answer is correct:

Dip one end in bubble mixture and start to blow bubble 1. Then dip the other end in mixture and keep blowing, to make bubble 2 (while, at the same time, enlarging bubble 1).

Grip the pipe in the middle by your thumb and fingers, making a fairly efficient seal, to connect the air inside both bubbles.

*The small bubble gets smaller and the big bubble gets bigger.*

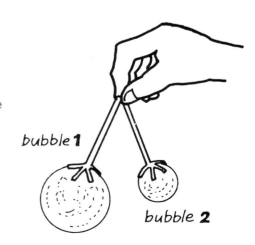

bubble **1**

bubble **2**

# Getting work from a bubble

To a scientist, "work" is something being moved – and that involves the use of energy. When you blow a bubble, air is forced to move against and to stretch a detergent film. Where does that energy go to?

Some of the energy goes into keeping the linings of the bubble envelope tightly stretched. Therefore a bubble stores energy in its surface tension (and also in the springiness of compressed air that it holds).

Can any of this stored energy be regained?

Put a candle in a dish of sand, for safety. Light it. Then blow a big bubble with your Super Bubble Pipe. If you take your finger or hand away from the mouthpiece, the elastic envelope of the bubble is allowed to contract – squeezing out the air.

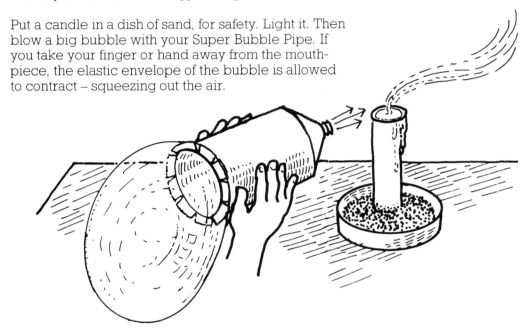

Energy that was stored in the filmy envelope is making the air move.

If you allow the airstream to hit the top of the candle, the flame is put out. Moving air does the work of forcing candle-wax vapor away from the hot wick and of so cooling the flame that it is destroyed.

## Challenge

Carbon dioxide gas in your breathed-out air also helps to extinguish the candle, but scientists have found that pure air alone does it too – although more time is needed. Perhaps you can invent a fairer way to do the test, by using a bubble filled with ordinary air. (For instance, you might connect a cardboard balloon-pump to your Super Bubble Pipe, using some tubing . . .)

# Bubble "power-station"

Diagonally fold a piece of paper measuring 4 x 4 inches, to make creases between the corners. Squeeze the creases to make an object that looks like this:

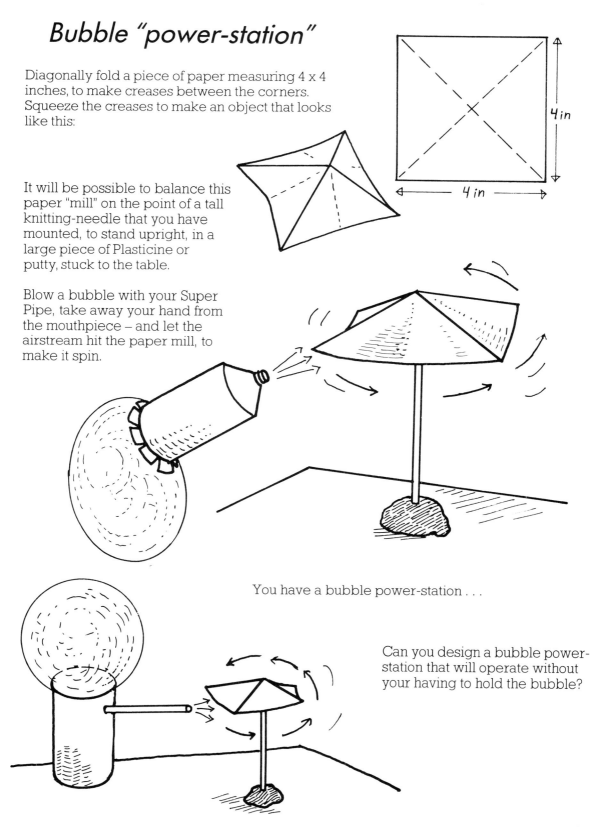

It will be possible to balance this paper "mill" on the point of a tall knitting-needle that you have mounted, to stand upright, in a large piece of Plasticine or putty, stuck to the table.

Blow a bubble with your Super Pipe, take away your hand from the mouthpiece – and let the airstream hit the paper mill, to make it spin.

You have a bubble power-station . . .

Can you design a bubble power-station that will operate without your having to hold the bubble?

# Bubble jet motors

## Motor: Mark 1

Bore a neat hole in one end of a rectangular plastic margarine pot. The hole must be big enough to admit the end of a peashooter – but not too tightly . . . . A good way to make the hole is to use a cork-borer (borrowed from a secondary school science teacher). Heat the cutting end of the cork-borer above a candle flame, before using it to partly cut and partly melt the hole.

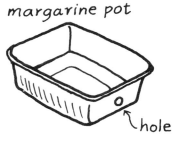

*margarine pot*

hole

Wet the pot with bubble mixture. Turn it upside-down and dip its "top" in the mixture, to catch a detergent film. Insert the peashooter in the hole – and blow a bubble.

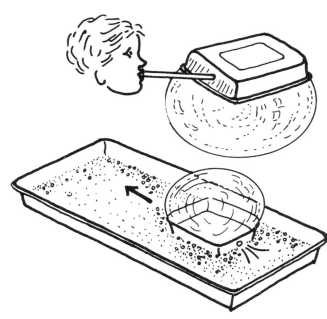

Carefully turn the pot and bubble upright. Remove the peashooter. Float the device on water in a tray. The "water" can, in fact, be the bubble mixture you use to make the bubble.

Slowly but surely the bubble deflates, pushing a jet of air from the hole – and this causes the boat to be driven by pressure on the opposite inside end of the pot.

## How it works

If the hole is kept covered, pressures on all parts inside the bubble (including the pot) are equal – and cancel out, and so the boat does not move.

If air is allowed to escape from the hole, the unbalanced force on the opposite inside end of the pot drives the little craft along. *Yes, this is really a jet-engine.*

*pressure inside bubble*

*air escaping*   *pressure inside bubble*

# Motor: Mark 2

Persevere with this model. It works beautifully if you work at getting it right.

Study the picture. The pillar in the center of the model is made from a pastic bottle with its top cut off, a plastic saucer, and a milk-bottle (don't let it break) standing upside-down. The slight hollow in the bottom of the bottle is useful.

The yogurt pot (motor) is stuck, with a large piece of putty, on one end of the bent wire. There is a weight hanging on the other end, as a balancing counterweight.

Notice the small hole in the upturned yogurt pot.

**You need:**

tall plastic bottle
with top cut off
plastic saucer
milk bottle
yogurt pot
wire
putty
bubble mixture in tray
peashooter
weight (e.g. small padlock)

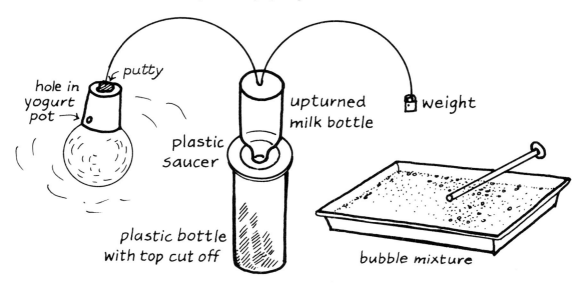

Remove the pot from the wire. Insert the peashooter into the hole. Dip the opening of the pot in bubble mixture. Blow a bubble and pull away the pipe.

Then, very carefully (you might need a helping hand), fix the hanging bubble and pot back on the wire.

As air escapes through the hole, the hanging pot and bubble are forced (by unbalanced pressure) to move slowly in the opposite direction. This "motor" should just about manage one complete circuit of the bottle.

Remember, persevere . . .

# Bubbles that bounce and fly

Put two equal bubbles, side by side, on separate stands. Bring the bubbles together and let them touch. Most likely, they will not stick together. You can even get them to bounce against each other, like soft boxers . . .

The tail ends of detergent molecules lining the outsides of these bubbles do not "like" each other – and so the bubbles can be bounced apart.

Bubbles do not stick to wool, and so a big bubble released over a blanket or carpet bounces when it hits the ground.

Two people wearing woollen gloves can "play ball" by patting a bubble to and fro between themselves.

Can you juggle with some small bubbles blown for you by a helper using a straw or peashooter pipe?

Do not make these bubbles too wet. Let surplus liquid drain and drip from the bubbles, before using them in the activities mentioned.

Bubbles are denser than air. Therefore they fall, unless they are carried away by breezes and gusts of wind. But a bubble can be made to hover in the rising hot air current above a kitchen hot-plate. (**Ask your parents to help you do this safely.**)

## Lift-off indoors

A more convenient way to fly a bubble is to provide a mobile engine in the form of a hand-held, battery-driven electric fan.

Start the fan working and put it aside on the table. Blow a big bubble and let it fall. Quickly take the fan beneath and watch the bubble wobble amazingly in mid-air, changing shape as it floats aloft.

Take a bubble "for a walk" across the room. Fly it above somebody's head, like a halo. Watch it go up higher as it evaporates and loses mass ("weight").

Admire the brilliant rainbow colors that brighten just before the bubble bursts, with a low hiss, in a gentle shower of spray.

Invent a game called "Bubble Tennis".

Two persons flying separate bubbles can have a race.

# CIRCUS OF BUBBLES
## ACT 1

A wet finger coming into contact with a bubble will penetrate its envelope. This is possible because the film of wetness covering the finger actually merges with the bubble's envelope. The trick works best when the finger is wetted with bubble mixture.

## Brave bubble

Blow a big bubble with the Super Pipe and put it on a tall stand, like the one described on page 24. A bright blue plastic bottle makes a splendid stand.

Wet a long, gaily-colored knitting-needle.

You can stab the bubble with the needle, and even push it through from one side to the other – "An arrow passing through its head" – without the bubble's breaking.

While the needle is penetrating the bubble, make some magical circular motions with it. Say "Hey Presto" and slowly lift the needle sideways through the top of the bubble – a flourish that looks impressive.

Finally, touch wet fingers with a friend – with fingers inside the bubble. These tricks are sheer magic to many people.

# Putting things inside bubbles

You need a brightly colored plastic toy, or a pottery animal. Dip the figure in bubble mixture and put it on the bubble stand.

Then, while you are holding the end of the Super Pipe just above the figure, blow a big bubble and let it merge with the wetness covering the figure – and move down to settle on the stand.

The effect of this technique is to trap the figure entirely inside the bubble.

---

An interesting toy consists of a short plastic stick with one wavy edge and a small propeller at the end. If the stick is held by one hand while a plastic rod is rubbed to and fro along the uneven edge, vibration causes the propeller to spin.

If the apparatus is wetted first, the propeller can be made to spin inside a bubble . . .

# CIRCUS OF BUBBLES
## ACT 2

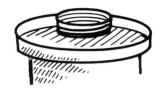

## A bubble within a bubble

Put a wetted bottle cap on top of a wetted bubble-stand.

Use a Super Pipe to blow a big bubble on the stand, trapping the bottle cap inside it.

Wet a peashooter. Dip it in bubble mixture, to catch a drop of the liquid. Then, insert the tube through the top of the large bubble – and blow a small bubble to settle on the bottle cap.

You have a bubble within a bubble – a great applause-getter in any Bubble Magic Show.

## A trick with electricity

Rub a polystyrene food dish (from a supermarket) with wool. This will charge the polystyrene with static electricity.

You can use this electrified object to attract a bubble and make it wobble . . .

# "Skipping" with a bubble

Blow a big bubble using a Super Pipe and attach the bottom of the bubble to a second (wetted) Super Pipe that is held by your other hand.

You will be able to stretch the bubble between the pipes.

Imagine that the pipes are handles of a skipping-rope. Give the pipes circular movements. You have a "skipping" bubble. . .

# Electrical mystery

Sometimes, if you have two identical bubbles hanging side by side and just touching, they can be made to go together as one. Bounce them a little. Get people around you to rub plastic objects with wool.

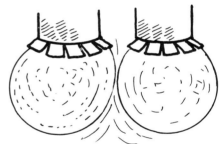

If the experiment works, it is wonderful to see. (Electricity is almost certainly involved in the explanation.)

# CIRCUS OF BUBBLES
## ACT 3

If you dip a peashooter or drinking-straw pipe into bubble mixture, and you poke the end of the tube in to the drop of liquid hanging from the bottom of a big bubble, you can blow a smaller bubble that will attach itself and stay there dangling.

## *Fat caterpillar*

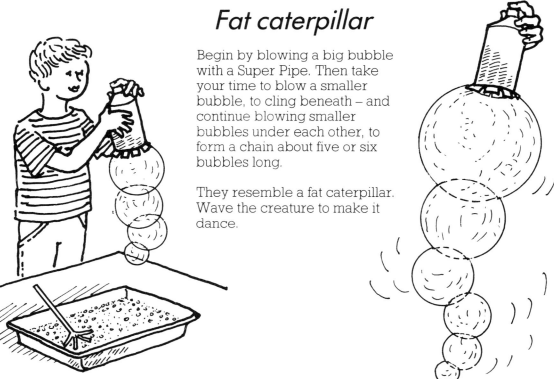

Begin by blowing a big bubble with a Super Pipe. Then take your time to blow a smaller bubble, to cling beneath – and continue blowing smaller bubbles under each other, to form a chain about five or six bubbles long.

They resemble a fat caterpillar. Wave the creature to make it dance.

You will need to practice this entertaining trick.

# Rotating bubbles

Make a chain of two big bubbles.
They should be about equal in
size.

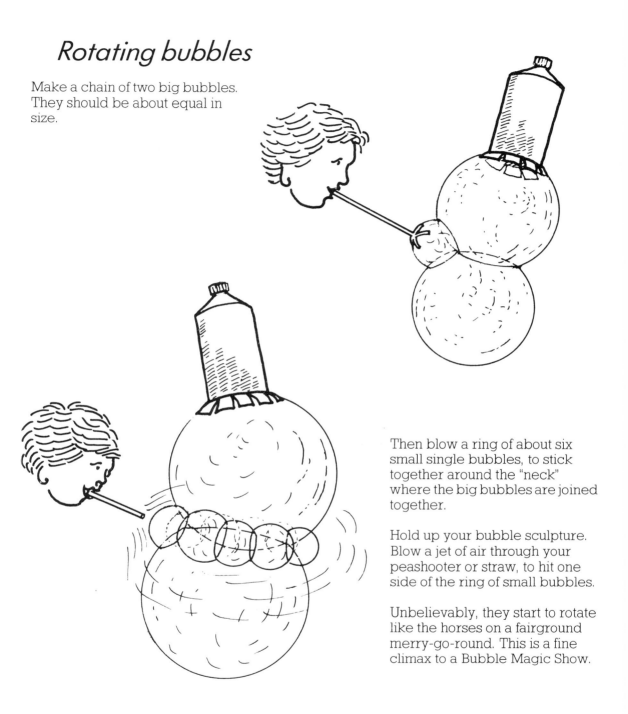

Then blow a ring of about six
small single bubbles, to stick
together around the "neck"
where the big bubbles are joined
together.

Hold up your bubble sculpture.
Blow a jet of air through your
peashooter or straw, to hit one
side of the ring of small bubbles.

Unbelievably, they start to rotate
like the horses on a fairground
merry-go-round. This is a fine
climax to a Bubble Magic Show.

You ought to be able to master this trick in about half
an hour.

# "Monsters" and domes

Put some bubble liquid in a large, watertight tray. Use your Super Bubble Pipe to blow a bubble. Let the bubble touch the surface of the liquid – and keep blowing. The bottom of the bubble spreads over the surface, to form a dome.

You should, by now, be expert at taking fresh breaths through your nose – to refill your lungs – without having to take your lips away from the pipe (from which hangs a bubble formed from your first breath).

It will be possible to blow a huge bubble dome that completely covers and swells above the tray.

Team-work makes this bubble activity more fun. Two persons using Super Bubble Pipes can cooperate, to produce a monster bubble over the biggest shallow dish you can find.

## *Bubble-inspired architecture*

The German architect Frei Otto uses actual bubble domes, a wind-tunnel and a computer, to help him to design cheap, strong coverings for large areas, such as sports stadiums, city centers and zoos. His tent-like structures are spun from fibre-glass six times finer than silk, but stronger than steel. They are suspended from steel cables on steel pylons. Frei Otto is "the father of tensile architecture". He designed the Arabian-styled cover for Hajj Airport in Saudi Arabia.

Inflatable buildings (that are kept in shape by air pressure) are constructed on bubble principles. An important way in which the study of bubbles can help the designers is to make it possible for them to see the weak spots in their ideas, before the full-size structures are built.

# Games and tricks with bubble domes

Bubble domes can also be created on formica-topped tables, well-wetted with the bubble mixture.

Invent fantastic bubble-domed buildings by forming clusters of bubble hemispheres.

Using a peashooter pipe, you can blow a bubble dome inside a bigger bubble dome made with your Super Pipe. The whole peashooter must be wet. Dip its end in bubble mixture, insert it through the main dome, and blow your shut-in bubble.

How many domes within domes (like a Chinese nest of boxes) can you create? This would be an exciting activity for a party competition . . .

Try rolling *wet* marbles through a bubble dome.

Roll the marbles through from opposite directions, letting them collide in the middle.

Make up some more bubble dome circus tricks.

# Bottled bubbles and foamy jumpers

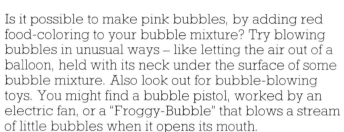

Is it possible to make pink bubbles, by adding red food-coloring to your bubble mixture? Try blowing bubbles in unusual ways – like letting the air out of a balloon, held with its neck under the surface of some bubble mixture. Also look out for bubble-blowing toys. You might find a bubble pistol, worked by an electric fan, or a "Froggy-Bubble" that blows a stream of little bubbles when it opens its mouth.

Fill a big bottle with your bubble mixture. Partly cover the top with your hand. Turn the bottle over, to let the liquid run out slowly into a bowl. Air goes up into the bottle and makes swarms of bubbles. You will have a bottle filled with bubbles when the mixture has drained away. Put a cork in the bottle. Study the shapes of the squashed bubbles. (Their arrangement is very mathematical.) Can you see any cubic bubbles? Observe what happens to your bottled foam.

Did you know that fragrant bath foam also helps to keep your bath-water hot? Hundreds of thousands of very tiny bubbles in the floating foam contain air cells that make it act like a woollen jumper – preventing heat from escaping very quickly from the water. You could test two lots of hot water in wide, shallow dishes – both starting at the same temperature and one covered with foam – to find out which gets cold first.

# Longer-lasting bubbles

When you buy a tub of bubble mixture, you often find that it contains a specially designed ring having a curiously wrinkled appearance. Its purpose is to hold extra liquid, so that many separate films – and bubbles – are produced.

Also, the bubble mixtures that you can buy are different in composition from your own detergent-and-water mixtures.

If you want your bubbles to last longer, you can try adding other substances, such as sugar solution and glycerine – to make the bubbles stronger.

You could carry out an investigation, involving different strengths of glycerine in your basic bubble mixture, to find out how long the bubbles you make will last, when placed on stands.

Perhaps you will want to measure the bubbles you make. One way is to let a bubble burst on a dry formica top, and to measure the diameter of the circular print that it leaves behind. Another way is to measure the width of a bubble on a stand, or of a hemisphere, by actually pushing a *wet* ruler right through it.

You can always discover new things about bubbles and invent new bubble tricks.

**Always cover your working surfaces with waterproof material, to avoid damaging them.**
(Sugar and glycerine are particularly messy . . .)

# Bubble art works

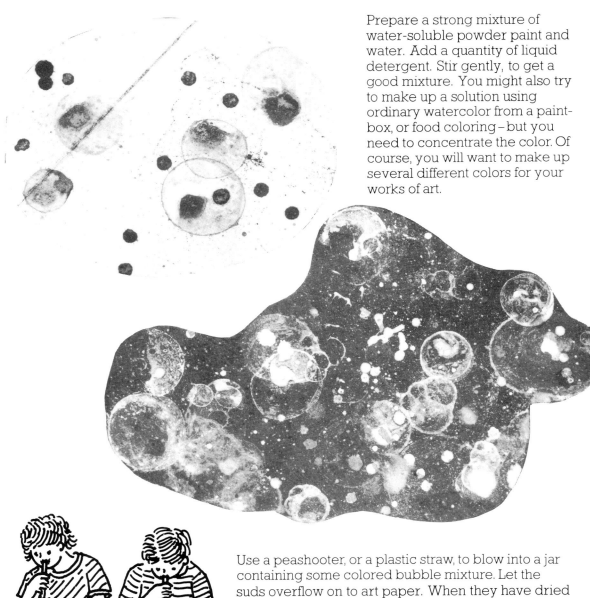

Prepare a strong mixture of water-soluble powder paint and water. Add a quantity of liquid detergent. Stir gently, to get a good mixture. You might also try to make up a solution using ordinary watercolor from a paint-box, or food coloring – but you need to concentrate the color. Of course, you will want to make up several different colors for your works of art.

Use a peashooter, or a plastic straw, to blow into a jar containing some colored bubble mixture. Let the suds overflow on to art paper. When they have dried they leave patterns like honeycombs.

Use a drinking-straw pipe to blow separate bubbles, allowing them to fall on to art paper. Use different colors to create fantastic pictures resembling planets, stars and suns in Outer Space.

Experiment with different strengths of added color in mixtures, to get fainter or darker bubbles in your art. Use your imagination. Invent different methods.

# Sculpture – a "snake" made from bubbles . . .

**You need:**

two or more 1-quart lemonade bottles
jug
bubble mixture
plastic tubing

You need a tall, transparent plastic pipe. Make it by telescoping two or more sections, obtained by cutting lengths from one-quart lemonade bottles (after getting their labels off).

The base section of this pipe will be an upside-down bottle with only its "bottom" end removed. The next section must fit neatly into the base – so be careful to cut a bottle at its top end, where it begins to taper.

Stand the pipe in a jug containing bubble mixture. A piece of plastic tubing (for example, from a wine-making kit) is passed down into the jug, next to the lip, and turned up, to go through the opening at the base of the pipe. This end of the tube must be submerged in the liquid.

Take a deep breath and blow steadily into the tube, to produce hundreds of bubbles that rise in continuous array. The bubbles rear out of the top of the pipe, before curling down and twisting together, like the coils of a fat serpent – fascinating to watch. . .

Play with the basic idea. Invent a better machine. How can you control the size of the bubbles generated?

# Index